For Asali, Sadie, Rafael, Stella, Margot, and Edie.

Text © 2022 by Helen Docherty
Illustrations © 2022 by Thomas Docherty
Cover and internal design © 2022 by Sourcebooks

Sourcebooks and the colophon are registered trademarks of Sourcebooks.

The full color art was created with acrylic ink on watercolor paper and composed and edited digitally.

Published by Sourcebooks Jabberwocky, an imprint of Sourcebooks Kids
P.O. Box 4410, Naperville, Illinois 60567-4410
(630) 961-3900
sourcebookskids.com

Cataloging-in-Publication Data is on file with the Library of Congress.

Source of Production: Wing King Tong Paper Products Co. Ltd., Shenzhen, Guangdong Province, China
Date of Production: April 2022
Run Number: 5025502

Printed and bound in China.
WKT 10 9 8 7 6 5 4 3 2 1

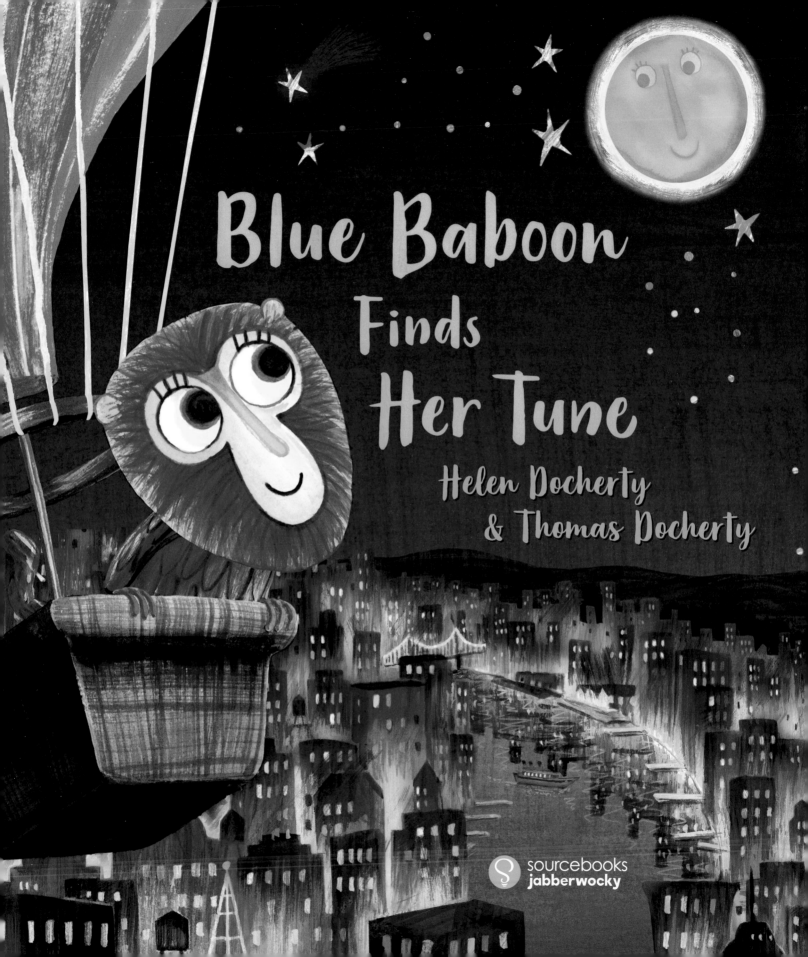

Blue Baboon
Finds
Her Tune

Helen Docherty
& Thomas Docherty

sourcebooks
jabberwocky

Orange moon,

blue baboon.

Blue baboon

spies bassoon.

Blue baboon plays bassoon

...out of tune.

Blue baboon.

Big monsoon!

Big monsoon,

wet baboon.

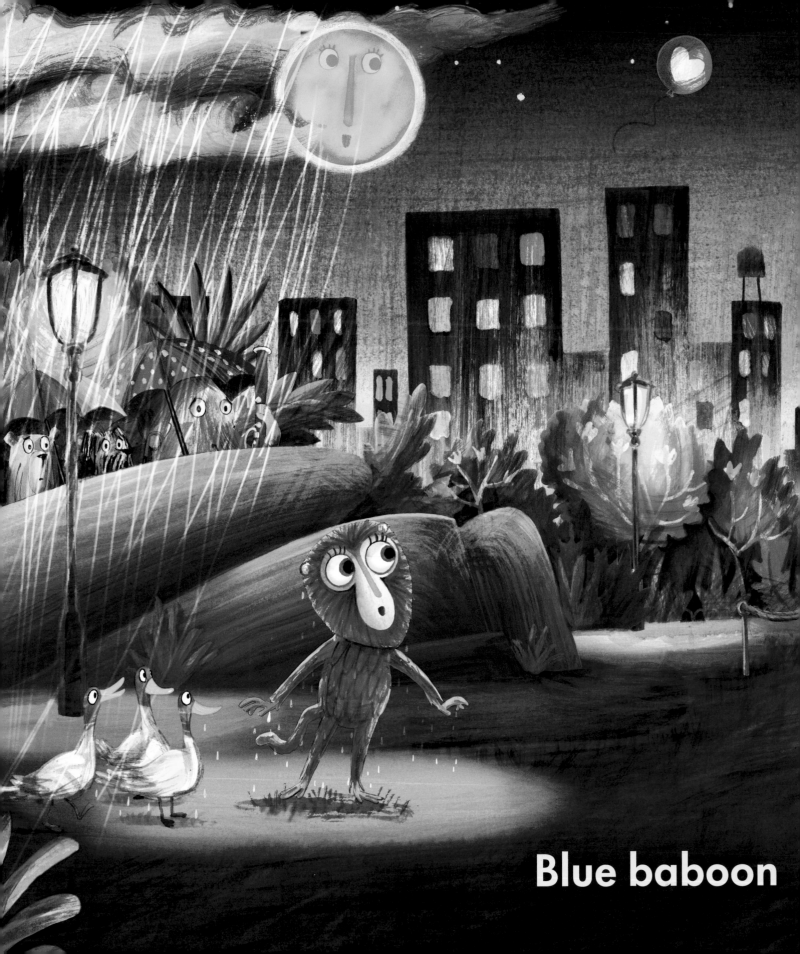

Blue baboon

finds balloon.

Blue baboon
leaving soon...

Blue baboon
takes bassoon.

Orange moon.

Blue baboon.

Blue baboon
lands on dune.

Blue baboon
plays her tune...

on the dune.

Green baboon
climbs the dune,

starts to croon...

...out of tune.

Orange moon,